Tyran

nosaurus Tex

Betty G. Birney

Illustrated by John O'Brien

Houghton Mifflin Company
Boston 1994

For my parents
and for Frank and Walshe
—B.G.B.

For Tess—J.O'B.

Library of Congress Cataloging-in-Publication Data

Birney, Betty G.
    Tyrannosaurus Tex / Betty G. Birney ; illustrated by John O'Brien.
    p.   cm.
    Summary: Tyrannosaurus Tex, a dinosaur cowboy, helps Cookie and
Pete put out a prairie fire and scare away some cattle rustlers.
    ISBN 0-395-67648-7
    [1. Dinosaurs—Fiction.   2. Cowboys—Fiction.]   I. O'Brien, John,
1953–   ill. II. Title.
Pz7.B5229Ty   1994   93-30727
[E]—dc20   CIP
                            AC

Printed in the United States of America

BP   10   9   8   7   6   5   4   3   2   1

"Stir the pot, Pete. They'll be a-coming in soon," said Cookie.

Pete stirred those beans till a cloud of dust drifted across the plain, followed by thundering hoofbeats, then whooping and hollering.

Pa and the cowboys from the Bar Double U were back from the roundup, back from a day of roping and branding cattle on the range.

"Hound Dog saw himself a monster out there," laughed Ham.

Cookie snorted as he filled Ham's plate. "Probably saw himself in a mirror."

"Old coot," muttered Hound Dog. "You're getting too old to beat a biscuit. And Pete's too young to bend a bean."

"Let's chow down," Pa said.

After the beans, the bacon, the biscuits and coffee were all gone, the boys sat around the campfire.

Ham told a story about a cowboy named Pecos Bill who rode a mountain lion and used a rattlesnake as his lariat.

Pete liked the story, even if Pecos Bill maybe wasn't real.

Next morning, while the boys went off to rope and brand, Pete picked rocks out of the beans and Cookie shined up the chuck wagon.

Twenty-three rocks later, Pete saw a cloud of dust drifting in. Then he heard thundering hoofbeats.

"Too early for the boys," said Cookie.

The land became darker with the cloud. Then it came, louder than thunder. "Howdeeeeeee!!!" it roared.

Pete looked up and up, and up some more. The thing was halfway as high as Butterfly Butte.

"Name's Tex. Tyrannosaurus Tex," said the creature. "And I've got a powerful hunger."

Cookie pointed to the pot of beans. "Help yourself," he said.

Tex opened wide and ate it, pot and all.

"Much obliged," said Tex.

"Any time," said Cookie.

Tyrannosaurus Tex had teeth as long and sharp as Cookie's best knife. And he wore the biggest cowboy hat Pete had ever seen.

"My ten-thousand-gallon hat," explained Tex when Pete stared at it.

Tex sat and talked friendly-like. Once Pete relaxed some, Tex gave him a ride atop the ten-thousand-gallon hat.

Pete sat up on the brim while Tex spun the hat around.

"Ya-hoo!" Tex bellowed.

Again there came a far-off thundering, then whooping and hollering. When the boys saw Tex, they skedaddled out of sight.

"He won't hurt you," Pete assured them.

The boys came back, quieter this time.

"Told you it was a monster," Ham said.

"Monster?" answered Cookie. "Boys, this here's just a big lizard. Everything's big here in Texas!"

Eating biscuits hot off the chuck wagon, the cowboys got used to Tex.
Tex talked about Texas before the people came.
He told how his friends disappeared, how the land flowered and
new animals came.

"There's always something new coming along. Or someone new."
Tex winked at Pete. "Like this fellow."

"You tyrannosauruses sure can spin a yarn," sighed Ham.

As they settled into their bedrolls, Pa told Pete, "I don't think we have
to worry about coyotes."

But they had other worries that night—lowdown rustlers set fire to the dry prairie grass, and the Bar Double U cattle ran wild in a stampede. The rustlers planned on stealing as many of the cattle as they could.

Pa and the boys rode like fury to try and save the herd.

"Why are they buzzing 'round like skeeter bugs?" Tex asked, puzzled. "Why don't they just put out the fire?"

"Closest water's clear on the other side of Butterfly Butte," Cookie told him.

Without a word, Tex stalked off. The tumbleweed tumbled. Even the sky seemed to shake.

The flames were three chuck wagons high when Cookie decided they couldn't wait for Tex to come back.

"Let's teach those no-count varmints a lesson," he said to Pete.

Cookie's gnarled old hands shook as Pete helped him lift a sack of corn off the chuck wagon.

"One . . . two . . . three!" counted Cookie as they tossed the sack on the
fire. "Now stand back!"

Lickety-split, that dried corn started popping like fireworks on the Fourth of July.

The rustlers thought the United States Cavalry had arrived. They high-tailed it out of there like they'd seen the ghost of Pecos Bill.

But before they got away, Tex came back and turned his hat over right on the flames.

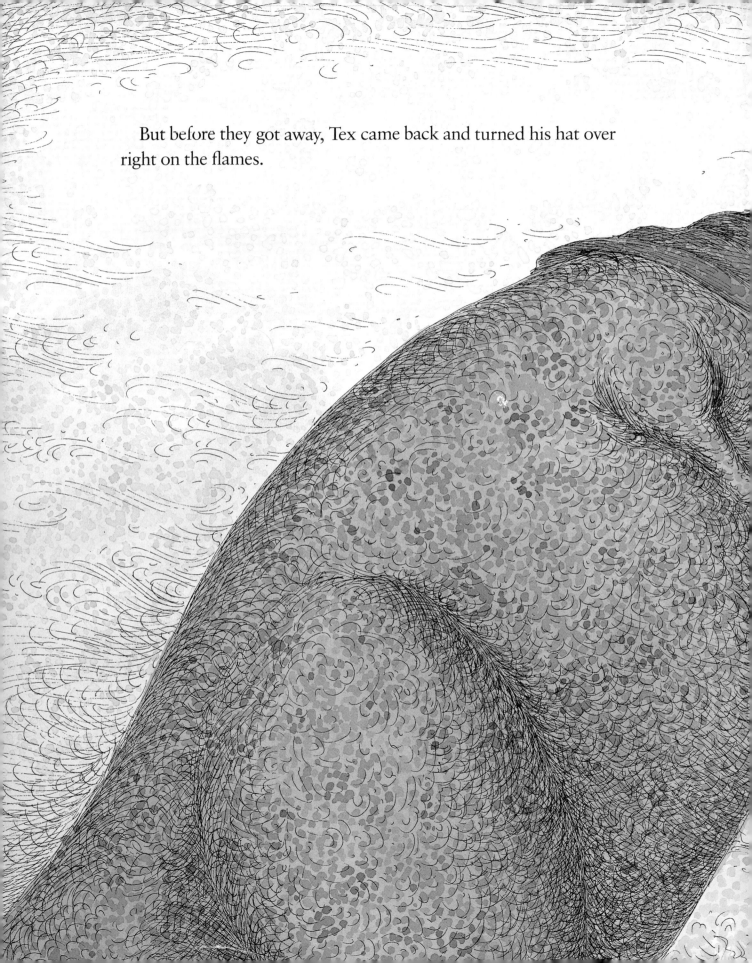

Ten thousand gallons of pure spring water poured over the fire!
The rustlers and their horses had to swim all the way to El Paso.

By the time the cattle came to their senses, they were safe and sound and rounded up again.

Pa thanked Tex and asked him to stay with the roundup.

"Sorry, partner," said Tex. "I gotta keep moving. But you got good help with these two youngsters."

He tipped that giant hat to Cookie and Pete.

And with a trembling of the tumbleweed and a shaking of the sagebrush, Tyrannosaurus Tex was gone.

Later, around the campfire, each of the boys told his version of Tex and
Cookie and Pete and the stampede.

It was even better than Pecos Bill, thought Pete. And this time, it was real.

At least as real as any tale told around a campfire can be.

Disney

PLANES

pi
kids®

publications international, ltd.

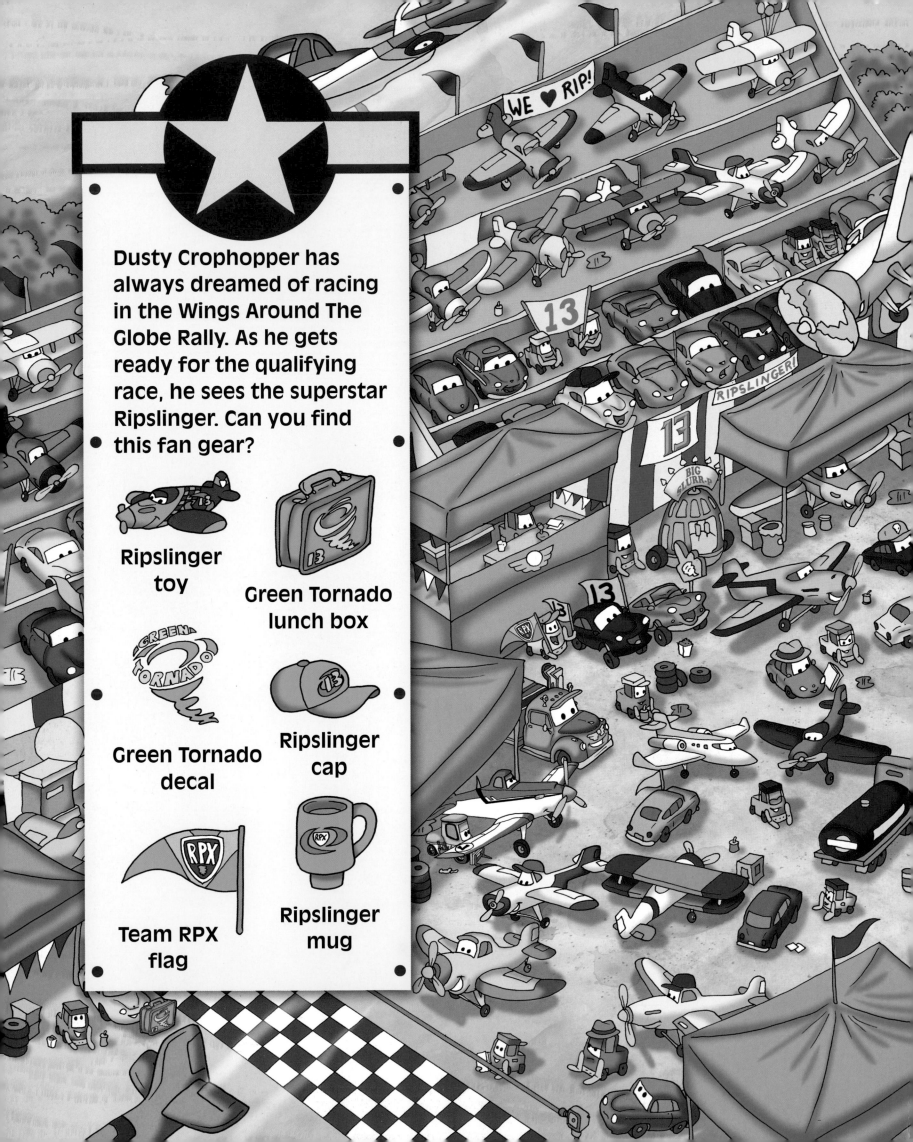

Dusty Crophopper has always dreamed of racing in the Wings Around The Globe Rally. As he gets ready for the qualifying race, he sees the superstar Ripslinger. Can you find this fan gear?

Ripslinger toy

Green Tornado lunch box

Green Tornado decal

Ripslinger cap

Team RPX flag

Ripslinger mug

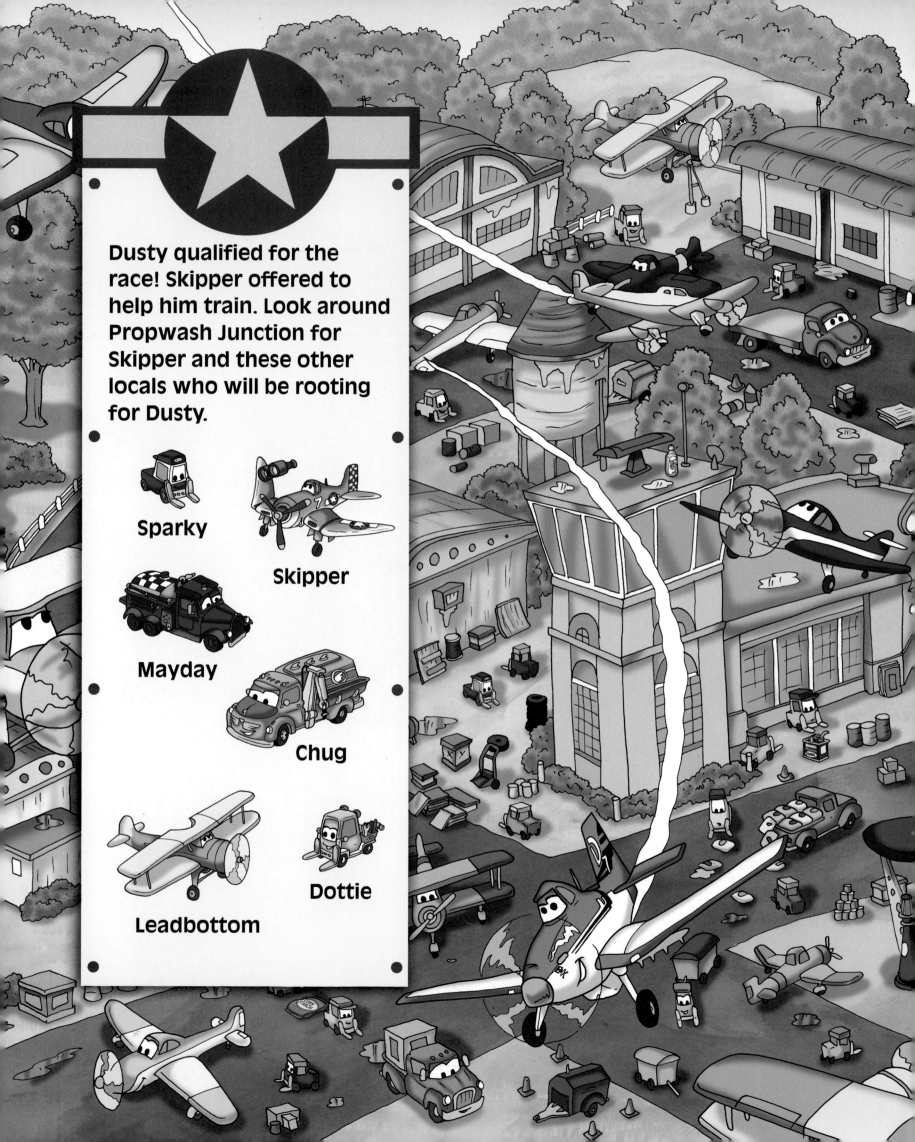

Dusty qualified for the race! Skipper offered to help him train. Look around Propwash Junction for Skipper and these other locals who will be rooting for Dusty.

Sparky

Skipper

Mayday

Chug

Leadbottom

Dottie

Franz is one of only six German cars that can transform into an airplane. Can you find Franz and the five others like him in the oil-hall?

While flying above the Garage Mahal, Dusty realizes he's a long way from home. See if you can find these things that make him homesick.

Skipper's star insignia

Tractor

American tourist

Can of ethanol

KERNEL
Premium
ETHANOL

Vita-minamulch sign

Chug look-alike

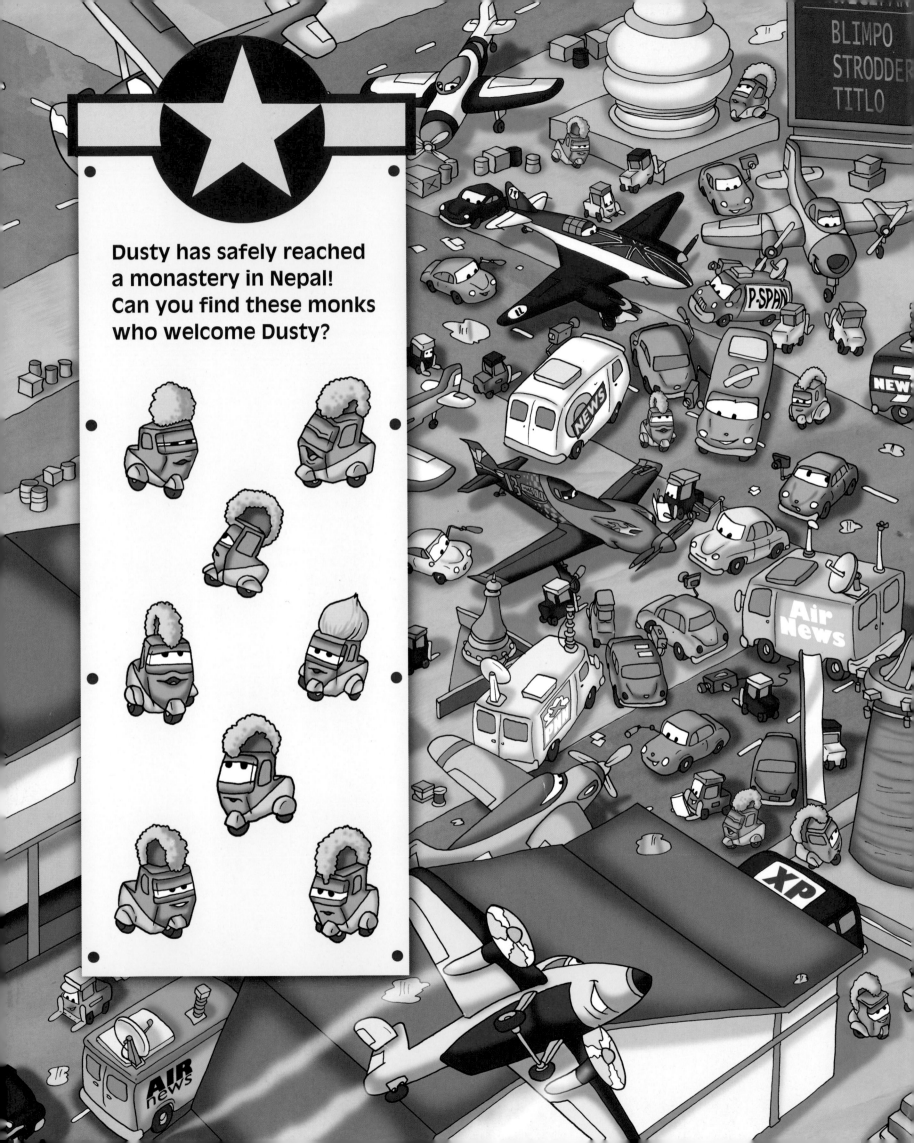

Dusty has safely reached a monastery in Nepal! Can you find these monks who welcome Dusty?

Dusty is getting some help from the Jolly Wrenches! See if you can find these members of Skipper's former navy squadron.

This shooter tug

This yellow gear tug

Bravo

This navy tug

This fighter

Captain

Echo

As Dusty gets ready for the final leg of the race, he needs to get fixed up. Will you find these plane parts that can replace his broken ones?

Propeller

GPS

Speed pump

Hydraulic pump

Flow control valve

Starter generator

Dusty has won the Wings Around The Globe Rally! Can you find his fans' favorite memorabilia?

Dusty toy

Crophopper flag

Dusty whistle

Dusty bobblehead

I'll Keep FLYING LOW

Poster

Dusty foam wings

Dusty hat

Dusty lunch box

Ned and Zed are twin planes known as The Twin Turbos! Fly back to the qualifying race and see if you can find them and these other pairs of twins.

Propwash Junction is a great place to live and work. Head back to town and find these products that are made there.

Can of ethanol

Bottle of corn oil

Bag of cornstarch

Tire

Spark plug

Windshield washer fluid

After a tough race, Dusty and El Chupacabra go to a German oil-hall. Can you find these flags from countries included in the Wings Around The Globe Rally?

Iceland

Germany

China

India

Mexico

USA

While Ishani shows Dusty around India, he realizes she is becoming his friend. Find these letters on planes at the Garage Mahal that spell "Ishani."